Amish Christmas

Homecoming

Samantha Bayarr
and **Sophia Grace**

Livingston Hall Publishers

Inspirational Books of Distinction

Table of Contents

Amish
Christmas
Homecoming

Samantha Bayarr
Sophia Grace

Chapter 1

Faith stepped off the warm, Greyhound bus clenching the letter her younger sister, Felicity, had written to her. Her letter had seemed urgent and she wondered if the girl had gotten herself into some trouble in the community that she didn't want their parents to know about. Faith had no idea if she could do anything to help the girl, but it was the only letter she'd written to her in the five years since she'd been gone, so she figured she should take it seriously.

Wearing the conservative dress that she never thought she'd be eager to wear again, the garment and headdress were both foreign and familiar, if that was possible. Icy wind whipped at the hem of her dress, and snow blew up around her knees causing her to grab her skirting and pull it tight against her thighs. It was Christmastime, and she'd missed the community almost as much as she missed her *mamm's* white Christmas pie. A horse-driven sleigh waited on the outer edge of the parking lot where it hadn't been plowed, and her heart pounded at the thought of riding home with Gideon.

She'd missed him most of all.

She smoothed back her hair without thinking. She'd been among the *English* too long. Gideon wouldn't care about her looks the way she did. She couldn't even be certain he would still be interested in her, but she prayed he would give her another chance and ask to court her. This time, she wouldn't turn him down. She was, after all, almost too old to be thinking of marriage. Her *daed* would tell her to think about taking the midwife position that she knew was open. Her *mamm* had written to her about it.

Being the community midwife was an option, but not one she preferred over having a husband and a family to raise. She'd missed farm-life and all the comforts of home. She'd missed it so much, she wasn't above humbling herself if need-be just so she wouldn't have to spend the rest of her life wondering if she should have married Gideon when she'd had the chance. In a lot of ways, she regretted leaving him that night, regretted her refusal to marry him *someday.*

Someday!

She hated the very thought of it. *Someday* had come and gone, but she was still painfully single, and certainly alone. She was no stranger to the loneliness that *English* life had left her with. It was a life she thought was so glamorous she'd abandoned all that was dear to her just to pursue it. It wasn't long after she'd run off before she realized what a mistake it was but then it was too late. One of her biggest fears was that the community wouldn't accept her back—that Gideon wouldn't accept her back.

She walked into the waiting area at the bus station, her coat buttoned up to the neck; Gideon stood in a corner with a far-off expression in his eyes, but when his gaze lifted her direction, her heart fluttered, but she couldn't be sure if it was out of love or nervousness. Faith and Gideon hadn't seen each other even once in the five years since she'd left the community. She'd been to school and experienced the world in a way he'd never known, but nothing could compare to the feeling of home, and that's just what Gideon was to her.

They stared blankly for what felt like an eternity, until Gideon finally stumbled his way across the room full of empty chairs to greet her. Like a true and honorable man, he removed his black felt hat and nodded, his soft blonde hair still showed highlights from working in the sun. His skin still held a nice golden color like it had when they were young, and would likely stay that way until March or April when the process would begin again. He was always the most sun-kissed in the peak of the summer, and it had always been very appealing to Faith.

As handsome as he'd turned out, she reprimanded herself for missing those years, but perhaps if she hadn't, she wouldn't be able to appreciate him now. Wasn't that the way it was supposed to be?

Oh, she'd missed him terribly, but now that she was face-to-face with him it wasn't as evident. She'd heard the expression; absence makes the heart grow fonder, but in this case, she couldn't be certain if it was true.

"Guttemayrie, Faith," he said softly, his nervousness obvious in his voice, but it was like sweet music to her ears. She'd put away the language when she'd left, but it suddenly seemed too foreign to return the greeting.

All their childhood, he'd had a crush on Faith and she'd broken his heart when she'd left the community after refusing to court him. They were childhood best friends though, and Gideon would never have turned down the opportunity to escort her home from the bus station. He was loyal to a fault, if loyalty could be considered a fault.

Faith glanced down, not really remembering how to act around Amish men. She managed to let out a little hello as Gideon scooped up her bags. It was awkward at best; not at all the feeling of home that she'd envisioned every time she'd rehearsed it in her mind. She knew he would be there for her but she somehow pictured their reunion a little differently in her head.

"I have a horse and sleigh out front. I know it's not really your style anymore but I hope it'll do." She tried to decipher his tone; in some ways, it sounded like he was joking, but there was an edge to his tone.

"Actually, a sleigh ride would be a nice change from the dirty cabs I've been riding in in the city the last couple of years," she answered. "Especially this time of year, it would seem almost magical. It's been too many years since we've taken a sleigh ride in the snow. I've missed that."

Faith quickly turned the other way, suddenly feeling embarrassed for having been so forward with Gideon. When she looked up she saw an Amish woman about their age getting into the only horse-driven sleigh that was parked in the large lot. She looked familiar to Faith but she couldn't quite place her.

She turned back toward Gideon, "Who is that in the sleigh?" she asked. She hadn't meant to sound so rude when she questioned him, but she felt a little disheartened thinking she'd have to share her sleigh ride with another girl.

"You don't recognize your own *schweschder?*" Gideon asked, his tone even stranger.

"She's all grown up!" Faith said. "I was surprised by her urgent letter but I had no idea she'd want to come to meet me today."

The last time Faith had seen her, she was an awkward pre-teen. She could clearly see she'd grown into a beautiful young woman.

"Felicity!" Faith called out to her, an eagerness to see her baby sister.

The girl hopped down from the sleigh and ran toward Faith, her arms wide open.

"Why didn't you come in out of the cold?" She asked.

"Because I wanted to surprise you," Felicity said, giggling.

"What a wonderful surprise it is!" Faith squealed like they did when they were younger.

Faith held her sister, tears, and laughter flowing from her at the same time. It wasn't the same greeting as she'd had with Gideon; this was much better. It was strange to her that things could be so awkward with Gideon, but, yet so natural with her little sister. Perhaps in time, Gideon would warm back up to her, though she figured he would have forgiven her after this much time had passed. In the meantime, she should enjoy the visit with her family and hope things would work themselves out with the two of them.

Faith stopped laughing for a moment to look at her sister. "You're all grown up! You have no idea how good it is to see you and how wonderful it was to get your letter, but what was it that was so urgent that you needed me home? You know I wasn't planning on coming home this Christmas since my new job starts January fifth."

"*Jah,* I know, but it just wouldn't be the same without you. Besides, I have so much to tell you," she said. "*Mamm* doesn't know I contacted you, so it's probably best if I fill you in a few things before we get back to the *haus*; that way you can make it look like a surprise."

"Now you have me worried," Faith said, and judging by her sister's sudden reserved demeanor, her heart sped up. "Is everything alright?"

Felicity shot a glance at Gideon and then forced a smile as her gaze met Faith's again.

Gideon helped both women into the sleigh and after placing Faith's luggage in the back, he climbed up on the other side of Felicity. His aloofness didn't go unnoticed by Faith, but she brushed it off, figuring he probably felt safer keeping some distance between them.

With a gentle snap of the reins, they were off toward the community that Faith had abandoned years ago. Her thoughts raced and she wrung her hands. Gideon took notice of her nervous behavior and offered some semblance of comfort. "You know Faith, everyone is excited to see you back home. We've all missed you a lot."

Faith's stomach did a little flip when he said they all missed her. Had he missed her too? She hoped so, having spent a lot of time over the years wondering about him before finally making the decision to return home.

She smiled weakly. "I guess I'm just nervous about returning to all my old ways, it's all so foreign to me. But at the same time, it's so familiar."

Gideon nodded and they remained silent for most of the trip, leaving Faith to feel a bit awkward. *English* life had led her to feel that conversations must always be flowing for people to be comfortable, but she knew Gideon didn't feel that way. She knew she could be quiet with him, but it still made her feel awkward after all these years.

She eased back into the buggy seat, trying to relax. She concentrated on the snow flurries twirling around in the cold winter air. That image had always mesmerized her and kept her calm. Maybe she would get the Christmas she had been longing for, like the ones from her childhood. She closed her eyes and said a silent prayer that it would be true.

After several more minutes of awkward silence between the three of them, Faith shifted in her seat and darted her gaze between her sister and Gideon. "How long do I have to wait before *one* of you tells me what's going on?"

Chapter 2

Gideon traveled down the same snow-covered alleyways he'd come since the plows hadn't made a pass in that direction yet. They made good time on the slick, country roads, bringing back memories of past sleigh rides that Faith thought she'd lost. Except for the fact that her now-older, baby sister, was along for the trip, it almost put her back there when she and Gideon were young and carefree without a worry in their own little piece of heaven on earth. She'd rebelled against Gideon, the community, and its ways; she'd wanted to continue her education so she could be something more than what her mother was—a *haus fraa.*

Felicity put a gloved hand on Gideon's arm in a way that hadn't gone unnoticed by Faith. "Slow the horse, *Gid*, I won't have enough time to tell Faith about *Daed.*"

Her calling him *Gid* had not gone unnoticed, but the mention of her father in such a way made her forget all about her sister's shameless behavior and she clenched the girl's arm.

"What about *Daed?* Did something happen?" Her lower lip quivered and her throat clenched as she watched the brightness in Felicity's blue eyes fade.

"He's had a heart attack," she blurted out, tears pooling in her eyes.

Faith felt the blood drain from her already cold face. "When?" she asked, barely above the jangling of the harnesses.

"In the middle of harvest season; Gideon stepped in and had to finish the season for him."

Faith's mind flashed to her mother's recent letters that had fallen off from their normal frequency. There had been a sadness in them she hadn't been able to explain; she'd assumed the woman was eager for her to finish school so she could return home. Now, she had to assume Felicity had called her home because she's a nurse; is this what God had in mind when she felt the calling to go to nursing school? She'd only just graduated; surely the fate of her father's life would not be placed in her hands.

"Is he bedridden?" Faith asked. "How long has he been down?"

Felicity lowered her gaze, pressed her gloved hands to her face, and began to sob.

"He seems to be getting weaker," Gideon said.

Faith's heart pounded so loudly she could hear it in her ears. "Why didn't someone send for me sooner?"

Felicity lifted her head from her hands. "We were waiting for you to graduate nursing school so you could help him," she sobbed. "I had no idea he would get this bad while we waited. I'm sorry."

Faith tucked her arm around Felicity's shoulders allowing her younger sister the liberty of sobbing. "I'll do everything I can to help him," Faith said. "But I've only just graduated and I haven't had any on-the-job training yet. I don't know what the rules are about acting as his nurse if I haven't clocked in any hours under my license for the experience."

"I understand all that," Felicity said. "But surely that doesn't apply to your own *daed.*"

Faith wasn't certain what the rules were, but the last thing she wanted to do was lose her license after all her hard work. Surely, she could help him; after all, lots of nurses worked on an in-care capacity. She looked at the hopefulness in her sister's eyes, realizing she expected a miracle from her she might not be able to deliver. The weight of her expectations filled Faith's gut with a sourness she'd never felt before, not even when she left the community.

Returning now to the community was such sweet sorrow; how could she possibly enjoy

Christmas with her family under such painful circumstances?

"I'll do what I can," she said. "But I'm not a doctor, and I've not had much experience yet. I know how stubborn he can be, but was he in the hospital yet or has he seen a doctor?"

Felicity nodded. "He was in the hospital two days before he demanded they let him out. You know how he is; he doesn't trust doctors—at least not the English ones."

"Wipe your tears, little sister, so that *Mamm* doesn't know you've been crying. I'll give her a chance to talk to me about it herself and I won't tell her you sent for me. Now let's have all smiles before we walk into the house," Faith said. "I'd like a nice reunion with the two of our parents; there will be plenty of time for tears later."

They stayed silent the remainder of the sleigh ride, but they clenched each other's hands for strength. As Gideon led the horse and sleigh into the Graber's driveway, Faith began to tense up again. She had managed to relax a little and even told herself everything would be okay the rest of the ride home; she'd watched the snow flurries and listened to the sleigh bells, but seeing her former childhood home sent a slight panic through her. Would everyone really be happy to see her as Gideon had suggested, or would her parents expect more from her than Felicity did?

She took a deep breath and stepped out of the carriage into the deep snow, sending a shiver up her spine and increasing the nervous goose bumps she already had. She blew out the breath with a whoosh, determined not to freak out when she saw her parents.

While she was helping Gideon get her luggage out of the sleigh, the front door to the Graber's home practically flew open. Faith looked up as her mother stepped out, and bounced through the snow to get to her. Her breath hitched when their eyes met; she'd aged, and it frightened Faith a little. The vulnerability in her mother's face caused her heart to skip a beat. Though she hadn't seen her in what felt like a lifetime, her smile was the same, and as she wrapped her arms around her, the feeling of home finally hit her.

"I missed you so much," her mother said. "How long have you been planning this visit without telling me?"

Faith giggled like a little girl because she felt like one at this very moment in her mother's arms. "I missed you too, *Mamm,*" she said. "Felicity invited me so I can surprise you, that's all *Mamm*, I promise."

Memories of past holidays rushed to her mind as the scent of cinnamon on her mother's apron tickled her nose. When she was younger, she always loved baking pies with her mother and the two would sneak out to build snowmen while the pies baked. They would laugh until they fell in the snow, where they would make snow angels.

One year, Gideon sneaked up on them with snowballs. They had the best time playing around in the snow that year. Her mother had always been more of a free-spirit than most Amish mothers; she was truly a kid at heart and gave Faith and Felicity the best childhood anyone could hope for.

Felicity pulled her into a robust hug, and then flashed her a strained smile as she pulled away. "You go and have some time with *Mamm* and *Daed,*" she whispered. "I'll help Gideon unhitch the team and give you a little time to visit."

Before she could say a word, her sister ran off toward Gideon and the sleigh.

"She's grown up so much," her mother said.

Faith raised an eyebrow. "I've noticed."

Faith's mind drifted as she watched Gideon and Felicity take the sleigh down the rest of the driveway toward the barn. There was a closeness between the two of them, but she shook it off as being a product of circumstances. He'd likely spent a lot of time over the past few months with her family, which would have thrown him and Felicity together more often than she felt comfortable with. She supposed she couldn't help but feel a twinge of jealousy at the thought of Gideon and her sister fishing in the pond by their houses, or shucking corn together, or playing in the snow—all things that she herself used to do with Gideon.

She and Gideon had done most everything together growing up, and the past five years without him had left her feeling lonely. Faith had always secretly thought she would marry Gideon, but when he asked to court her when they got a little older, she was scared. She thought she may want a different life, and with her *rumspringa* approaching at the time, she thought it would be her opportunity to find out. What she found out was that she should have never left home in the first place, maybe then she'd be the one still in that sleigh with Gideon instead of Felicity. Perhaps she'd have *kinner* of her own by now. It was obvious the closeness they once shared had been a closeness he now shared with Felicity.

Faith shook away her worries as she walked into the house with her mother. The sight of her childhood home and the smells of her mother's cooking in the kitchen brought back a sense of warmth for Faith. Living in the city, her apartment was shabby and never felt like home. Without her mother around, she never had the motivation to cook, she had missed the feeling of home more than anything.

She looked around but there was no sign of her dad. She wanted to ask without hurting her mother. She already knew the woman could see it in her eyes; she knew her too well.

Her mother sighed. "Felicity told you, didn't she?"

Faith nodded.

"He's upstairs taking a nap," she said. "He does that in the afternoons now—doctor's orders."

"When's the last time he saw his doctor?"

Her mother began to fuss with the dishes, putting away her taking utensils. She had taught her daughter to clean the kitchen while they waited for things to cook or bake, and Faith could see she hadn't changed.

"Gideon took him on Monday," she said over her shoulder.

That explained a lot of things. It was obvious to her that Gideon had stepped in as the head of her family and she wasn't sure how she felt about that just yet. It seemed that her family had experienced some growing, which left Faith feeling as if she'd grown apart from them—especially Gideon.

Chapter 3

Faith tiptoed into the room where her father slept peacefully. Though she didn't want to disturb him, she was eager to visit with him. She'd missed him dearly and it saddened her to see him so weak and vulnerable. She sat quietly at his bedside listening to him snore lightly. A lump clogged her throat and tears threatened to spill, but she bit the inside of her cheek to quell her emotions. The door opened a little, and the familiar squeak made Faith laugh inwardly. She would listen for that squeak every time she'd sneak out of the house to meet her friends when her *rumspringa* had first begun. It seemed funny to her how such a little thing mattered so much back then.

Her mother poked her head in the door and held up two cups, nodding to Faith.

She beckoned the woman into the room, rising from the chair so her mother could sit.

She shook her head. "*Nee,* I've spent too many hours in that chair watching him sleep; it's nice to see you there."

She held one of the cups toward her daughter, and Faith eyed the whip cream dollop and the nutmeg sprinkles. How did her mother know she'd wished for a cup of her wonderful hot cocoa to warm her bones?

Either she was getting too old for sleigh rides or they would take some getting used to again. She hoped Gideon would take her again soon, but she figured it might take him a while to warm up to her. Then, there was the apology she owed him for running out on the baptism and marrying him the way he'd hoped she would, and she would offer it fast— as soon as she could get a moment alone with him.

That was certainly not a subject she wanted to approach with her family watching and listening.

They sat together in silence for some time, Faith resting her head on her mother's shoulder after she grabbed a spare chair from across the hall. Thick snow blew in swirls in front of the window, the wind whistled through the tiny cracks in the windows of the old house. Laughter from outside reached her ears; it was quiet at first, but then it turned louder until she could hear her sister's squeals the way she would act when the two of them would have a snowball fight. Faith rose from the chair and crossed to the window, looking down on the large expanse of land between the house and the barn. She sucked in her breath as she watched Felicity and Gideon tossing snow at each other in a mock fight. They seemed very close, but surely, it was a brotherly and sisterly kind of closeness; surely her own sister would not betray her with Gideon.

Faith tossed around trying to wake up early to help her mother with the chores; she'd been so exhausted, she'd fallen asleep right after her one-sided visit with her father. The sun hadn't even come up yet and she'd had a restless sleep, but she hadn't been able to rid her mind of the image of her sister and Gideon carrying on in such a cheeky manner yesterday. She'd kept to herself most of the remainder of the day, and had even excused herself from the dinner table, using her father's care as an excuse to leave the festive attitude at the dinner table thanks to having Gideon as their guest.

She supposed her mother had fed him many meals in exchange for the help he'd given them in her father's absence. But it seemed like more than that—almost as if he'd become part of the family. She reasoned that it might make things easier once she accepted Gideon's proposal and the two were married.

She shook the sleepiness off and hopped out of bed, eager to work at her mother's side. She could already smell the slightest hint of cinnamon over the strong aroma of bacon and fresh coffee, meaning her mother had been hard at work preparing her favorite cinnamon bread for the morning meal. Mealtime was another thing she dearly missed while living in the city, where most of her meals were quickly prepared in a microwave. She'd gotten used to the fast-food world, but there was nothing more precious to her than spending hours in the kitchen next to her mother preparing real food that tasted sweeter on the tongue than the thickest honey from the groves at the far edge of her parent's property. There was something to be said for a home-prepared meal that was cooked slowly—simmering long enough to preserve the love in it.

Faith hurried downstairs after slipping her work dress over her head and pinning back her hair and tying a scarf at her chin. Donning an apron, she washed up and kissed her mother on the cheek before helping her mother stir, drain and pour breakfast.

Where was Felicity? Surely, she helped her *mamm* in the kitchen, but perhaps she was tending to her father's chores outside.

She stole glances at her mother, her heart warming up at the loving way her mother prepared breakfast. She'd missed little moments like this— moments she'd taken for granted before she left. She never thought she'd miss what she thought were such small moments, but she now realized they were her happiest moments, being home with her family.

Faith noticed her mother watching her from the corner of her eye. "Is something the matter?" she asked, chuckling lightly when Faith made a silly face the way she used to as a child.

Faith smiled. "No, nothing's the matter at all. I just missed being home, I missed you."

Faith's mother smiled and pulled her in for a hug. She knew the woman was happy to have her daughter home after five long years without her;

there were times Faith wondered if she would ever come home.

"I know I've missed so much while I was gone; I'm sorry I wasn't here when *Daed* suffered his heart attack." Faith's expression suddenly turned a little sad.

Although she was being reminded of all the happy moments she missed, she was also being reminded that she missed a lot of opportunities, like marrying Gideon and starting a family. Now she feared she may remain alone as a midwife and a spinster. Not that she had anything against midwives; her own birth had been tended by one of the best she could imagine, but that was never the life she wanted for herself. Looking at her mother, she was reminded of how she longed to be like her when she was growing up, with a loving family.

Faith's mother caught her expression changing. "Well now something's the matter, tell me what it is."

"I just fear I'm too old to be starting over here. I missed out on so much, I may never find a husband and be able to start a family like I've always wanted."

Frau Graber cupped her hands around her daughter's face. "You've got plenty of time to worry about such things; you're still young. A *gut mann* will come along and ask your *daed's* permission to marry you."

Her thoughts turned to Gideon and the night she'd left home. He'd threatened to go to her father and ask to marry her if she didn't make up her mind. She'd made up her mind in the other direction—a direction he hadn't planned for.

Was her mother trying to tell her to move on and find someone other than Gideon to marry?

Her mother swatted at her bottom playfully. "Go to the barn and get me a dozen eggs so I can scramble them quickly. The bacon is almost done."

Faith nodded as she picked up her winter coat from the peg near the back door and pushed her arms into the sleeves. That's when she noticed an extra plate at the table. Hope filled her heart at the thought of her father taking the morning meal with them and saying the blessing over the food. Spending more time out of bed would help him gain his strength back a lot faster than bringing him soup, and she would find a way to relay that to her family.

Faith shouldered out into the snowy morning, the wind whipping at the hem of her work dress. She found Gideon in the barn mucking out the stalls while Felicity busied herself feeding the horses. Giggling turned quiet as she approached and grabbed an apple from the barrel in the corner.

"What's so funny?" Faith asked her sister as she offered the apple to her horse and nuzzled his soft, velvety nose.

Felicity waved a hand at her. "Gideon was just telling me another funny story."

Faith nodded. "I just came out to get some eggs for breakfast; *Mamm* said it'll be ready as soon as she gets the eggs scrambled up."

"Tell her we'll be there in a minute," Felicity said, putting the lid on the grain barrel.

Faith looked back. "We?"

Felicity giggled. "Gideon can't cook his own breakfast until the repairman fixes the stove in the *dawdi haus.*"

Faith turned her back to her sister and walked toward the other end of the barn where the hens roosted. Her legs felt wobbly and her breath hitched. She knew Gideon had been helping her family with some of the chores since her father was too ill to do them, but why had no one told her Gideon was living in the *dawdi haus?*

Chapter 4

Faith felt suddenly apprehensive about having Gideon so close, even though she knew her mother needed a man to do the heavy chores while her father recovered. Still, she worried about the weak feelings she had for Gideon and the feelings he no longer seemed to return. She suspected there was something between him and Felicity, however innocent or serious it might be, and it made her want to avoid him as much as possible. She prayed the bad feelings would fade, but now that she would have to see him every day, she didn't see a way to steer clear of him.

One way was to spend as much time with her father as possible.

When she entered the dark room, she immediately went over to the window and pulled up the shades. She knew it wouldn't do him any good to sit in a dark room. Natural light was the best thing to lift his spirits, and to get him out of the bed. Her father lifted his head from the pillow and smiled at her.

"*Wei ghetts, Dochder,*" he said.

"*Guten morgen, Daed,* I'm *gut,*" she answered with a smile. "What do you say we get you out of this bed today and into the kitchen for the evening meal?"

He nodded vigorously. "*Jah,* that sounds like a *gut* idea for sure and for certain."

"Your color is nice and your blood pressure is normal," she said, kissing her father on the top of his head. "I don't see any reason why we can't get you up to sit with us for supper. Do you need Gideon to help you up?"

It made her cringe to even ask.

He shook his head. "He had to help in the beginning, but I've been able to get up on my own for a while—but they won't let me. Now with you here—on an official capacity as a nurse, maybe they'll listen to you. If they had their way, I'd stay in this bed for the rest of my days. Gideon's been a big help, but I need to start doing a little bit for myself."

"I agree," she said with a smile.

He smiled back. "*Jah,* that Gideon is going to make a right *gut* son-in-law."

Faith could feel the blood draining from her face. Did he think she was automatically going to be married to him because she returned? That would be up to Gideon, and he'd been so aloof in the past two days, she wasn't certain about anything anymore. But if it would please her father, she would try to reconnect with Gideon; she cared for him, but her feelings were in a state she didn't know how to describe. Perhaps in time, she would figure things out; her main concern was her father's health. There would be plenty of time to iron things out with her own future later.

Picking up his Bible, Faith read to him from Psalms—his favorite. About midway through, he closed his eyes, and though she had no idea if he was drifting off to sleep, she continued to read.

Around mid-morning, her mother came into the room to relieve her. Faith excused herself to go tend to the kitchen chores, but her mother stopped her.

"I've finished up everything in the kitchen," she said. "Your time might be better served in the barn with your *schweschder.*"

Her father usually required his medicine and some breakfast at this time, so she stepped aside to allow her mother to take over.

"Gideon can help refresh your memory of how to take care of the horses," her mother continued.

Faith's stomach did a little flip at her mother's statement; she was capable of tending the animals and didn't relish the idea of being left alone with Gideon. She especially didn't like the idea of him telling her what to do. In some ways, her mother had let him take over things around here, and for some reason she couldn't pinpoint, it bothered her—a lot.

Faith simply nodded to her mother, humoring her dependence on Gideon, and left the room so she could care for her father in private.

For the second time that morning, she found herself bundling up in her thick, wool coat to go out to the barn to be in close quarters with Gideon. She wished she knew what it was that made her feel like an intruder in her own life, but there was something to her uneasiness. He'd developed a closeness with her family that she'd lost when she left, and perhaps she was a little envious of his connection with them—especially Felicity.

Closing the barn door behind her, she glanced over at Gideon dolling out hay to the horses, and couldn't help but feel a tinge of sadness. Had she never left town, maybe she would be courting him and perhaps they'd even be married by now. Faith thought how perfect he was for her, being that he clearly cared for her family as if they were his own, but was that enough?

Gideon offered her a brush. "If you give him a *gut* rubdown he'll be ready for the harnesses," he said, showing her how to groom the horses.

She playfully took the brush out of his hand. "I remember how to groom a horse." She chuckled. "The horses were always my favorite." She nuzzled the gelding's nose.

Gideon smiled at her. "I'm happy to see that city-life hasn't changed you too much. We think it's wonderful *gut* to have you home," he said, looking down to hide the blush on his cheeks.

Faith tried to hide her smile. Had he meant that it was he who was glad to see her and not the horses? Or was he just trying to make her feel welcome? Faith didn't want to entertain the thoughts much; she knew that Gideon was needed in her family now, and she had to respect that.

The two went about the rest of the morning chores in silence, but her mind was far from quiet.

Faith couldn't change how much time had passed or how many things she'd missed by leaving home. She just knew things would be so different had she stayed. She'd be married and starting a family of her own, wouldn't she?

Felicity entered the barn and eyed Faith, making her feel almost uncomfortable.

"You two seem awfully cozy," she said. "I thought you'd be in tending to *Daed* instead of out here. Gideon and I can take care of what needs to be done here; you should go back in and take care of him."

Her tone hadn't gone unnoticed by Faith, who wondered if the girl regretted her decision to call her home to care for their father. Faith looked at her sister, wondering if her worry over their father had caused her sudden change in her attitude.

"*Mamm* asked me to come out here," Faith said. "I'm not needed in there right now; I thought I was needed out here, but I guess I was wrong."

She set down the grooming tools and flashed Gideon a look of disappointment and then left the barn without a word to her sister.

The next day, Faith and Felicity set out to the Yoder's house with their mother, where some of the women in the community were meeting for a quilting bee. The quilt was to be for Faith's childhood friend, Katie, who was soon to have a baby. While Faith was happy for Katie, she still felt a bit envious that her friend was married and having her first child while she was feeling out of place in the community.

The entire ride there, Felicity sang Gideon's praises. It was obvious Felicity had a crush on Gideon; that was going to be awkward between them when she got back together with him. It made perfect sense; the flirting and giggling, the time she hung around him. Not to mention, the jealousy when she'd found Faith in the barn with him. She would never say anything to embarrass her sister, but she knew she couldn't let it go on any longer; surely, Felicity's heart would be broken when she and Gideon resumed courting, and Faith didn't want to see her sister hurt over a crush. This dilemma gave her new reason to avoid Gideon—at least for now. She would put her concentration on spending more time with her sister to ease her away from him. She'd already decided to keep her distance for the time-being, trying to allow him space, and not wanting the constant reminder of what she'd given up, in the event he wouldn't take her back.

Faith decided to make the best of it and smiled politely with Felicity; she wouldn't confront the girl for risk of embarrassing her, and knowing Felicity, she'd only deny the crush and it would put a wedge between them. Her sister knew well of her past with Gideon and his attempts at courting her before she'd left for the city. Because of that reason alone, Felicity would never act on her crush; to do so would break the *sister code.*

"*Wilkum,*" Katie said to her, pulling her into a hug. "I've missed you."

Tears welled up in Faith's eyes as she looked at her very-pregnant friend. "I've missed you too; I missed your wedding, and now this! I'm so sorry I haven't been back, but I knew if I came back to the community I would never finish nursing school."

Katie smiled and rested a hand atop her swelling abdomen. "You're here now, and from what I hear of your *daed,* I would have to say *Gott* smiled on you with your education to help him mend. Perhaps you can assist the midwife when it's my time," she said.

Faith's heart pounded; her class had been present for a couple of births, along with other things such as surgeries, and even an autopsy, but she wasn't qualified to help birth a *boppli* on her own.

"My prayer has been that we could have a nurse in the community because the doctor is not always available," Katie continued. "You are much needed here."

"*Mei mamm* told me about the opening when Belinda marries, but I'll have to be in prayer about that," Faith said. "I'm so glad I could be here for your quilting bee."

Katie smiled. "Me too. Did you see the beautiful wedding ring quilt we did for Felicity last week for her dowry?"

Faith felt faint. She wanted to ask what her sister needed with a wedding dowry quilt, but by the time she found her voice, Katie's mother was calling her to sit so they could get started on the quilt. She glanced at her sister, who suddenly averted her gaze; was there something she wasn't telling her? She would find out in due course; for now, she was going to enjoy her visit with Katie; she hadn't been to a quilting bee in so many years, she hoped she hadn't lost her stitching talents.

The ride home from Katie's house was quiet. Faith filled her mind with the quietness of the country road blanketed in snow, and the sounds of the clip-clops from the horses' hooves—things she'd missed while she was away. It had been tough for her not to feel out of place at the bee—especially since she was unbaptized and unattached. Though the others did not reject her, she felt separate from the others; even Felicity had been baptized recently. She'd written to her about it. Her letter had told her she planned to stay in the community, marry and raise her family here. Had that letter been a precursor to her visit?

She wanted so much to say something to her mother and sister, but what could she say that wouldn't come out sounding like an accusation? Most of the youth courted in secret, and her questions could expose her sister's plans before an announcement could be made. She'd been away from the community too long for any of her questions to come out sounding like anything other than prying. She would have to be tactful and keep her eyes and ears open for clues.

Felicity had always been clumsy at hiding her emotions and thoughts; they used to share everything, but since she'd been back, the girl had kept a tight-lip on whatever it was she was hiding from her. She would find out the reason for her wedding ring quilt if she had to be rude and ask her outright.

Chapter 5

When they returned home, Gideon was finishing up the evening chores in the barn. Faith decided she should go talk to him about Felicity, since the girl had an obvious crush on him, and she feared her sister would get hurt when he rejected her.

Since he wasn't going anywhere anytime soon, she couldn't handle feeling any more awkward than she already did with her own family. She trekked out to the barn and her heart fluttered when she saw Gideon nuzzling her favorite horse's nose. She always loved how gentle he was with the animals. She shook away any adoring thoughts she had and made her way over to him.

Gideon looked up at her; she tried to hide her troubled heart with a forced smile, but he called her out before she even got the opportunity to speak, "I always could read your facial expressions," he said. "Is something wrong?"

Faith took a moment to gather her words; she didn't want to come off as rude and offend Gideon, but she had to spare her sister a broken heart. In her head, she chose her words carefully; the last thing she needed was for him to quit on her family because she offended him. "I just wanted to ask you about Felicity," she began, already sensing the awkwardness. "I've noticed some *changes* in her—and in you that I'm not sure how to read."

Gideon remained quiet.

"I realize that you've been here for a few months, and I'm sure you've developed a *closeness* with my family members," she said. "But it just seems that Felicity has become—well—clingy with you."

He scooped oats into the feed box and looked up. "Do you have a point to make, because I have work to do."

"I'm worried about her getting her heart broken," Faith said.

Gideon pulled off his hat and raked his fingers through his hair, blowing out a heavy breath that sounded angry. "And what makes you think I would do anything to break her heart?"

She forced a nervous giggle. "I'm thinking it would break her heart when she realizes you're not interested in her," Faith said firmly.

He plunked his hat back on his head and crossed his arms over his muscular chest. "So, what makes you think I shouldn't be interested in Felicity?"

Faith scrunched up her face and narrowed her eyes at him. "Well, are you?"

Just as Gideon was about to respond, Felicity walked into the barn.

She glanced between Gideon and Faith. "I just came out here to see if you'd like some warm cookies, Gideon," she said with a smile.

Faith knew that smile; she was smitten, and he seemed to be leading her on. It made her sick the way he was encouraging her with the smile and nod he returned her way. She wanted to give him a verbal reprimand, but to do so would only embarrass her sister, so she held her tongue.

"I'll be there as soon as I put the tools away," he said.

Felicity shivered, having walked out there without her coat. "Don't keep me waiting," she said very flirtatiously.

It irritated Faith to listen to the two of them carry on. It was almost as if …oh! That was even too preposterous to even entertain such a thought. Honestly speaking, she hadn't even acknowledged Faith, and hadn't invited her to partake in her baked treat she offered Gideon. Was the girl trying to win him over with her baking skills? Even at a young age, Felicity could out-bake her; she seemed to have a gift for making melt-in-your-mouth baked goods while everything Faith baked burned or dropped in the middle.

Much to Faith's dismay, Felicity seemed to have no intention of leaving despite the fact she was cold. Instead, she took a seat on the workbench in the barn and stared at them. "I'll just wait for you to finish up here so you can escort me back along the slippery trail."

Faith could sense the fakeness in her voice. She had dealt with girls who acted helpless to get attention while she lived in the city, girls much worse, but she could sense what Felicity was doing nonetheless. Faith didn't want to step on Felicity's toes, she only wanted her to respect her past with Gideon, and give her a chance to explore the possibility of rekindling it without the awkward possibility of competition from her own sister.

Gideon shrugged off his coat and slipped it around Felicity's shoulders. "I don't want you catching a cold while you wait," he said. "I'll make sure the path is freshly shoveled so you don't have to worry about slipping. I hadn't had a chance to get to it yet since it started snowing."

Faith practically choked at the forward but chivalrous behavior from Gideon toward her sister. Was *she* the reason he was so aloof toward her since she'd returned? She hadn't had a chance to talk to him about it despite her own feelings toward him, but she didn't know how much longer she could keep quiet about her sister's behavior. The way Felicity came off made her seem like the opposite of the kind of girl Gideon always said he had wanted to marry. So, why was he paying so much attention to her?

Faith smiled politely and excused herself from the barn. "We can talk later, Gideon." She said it mostly to get under Felicity's skin, knowing if she could get a reaction out of her, it might open the door for the two of them to talk. She started to walk out of the barn when Felicity jumped up and was on her heels.

"Wait," she said. "I'll go with you!"

After they were out of earshot, her sister took the bait. "What exactly do you mean, you'll talk to Gideon later? What were you two talking about?"

Faith never liked to lie, but she was in an awkward position. She wanted to get along with Felicity, and she didn't want to embarrass her. "Oh, it was nothing, I just had some questions about tomorrow's chores."

Whenever Faith lied, her voice squeaked like it did just now, and her whole family knew her *tell*. There would be no getting around it or trying to convince her sister to let it go at that. Felicity could always sense it by the way she crossed her arms and squinted her eyes—the way she was doing now.

"I'm trusting that you're being honest with me about Gideon, but I sense something is going on that I don't know about."

"I could say the same thing about you, Felicity!" she said. "Something is a little off with Gideon; I'm not too sure I like the two of you being in each other's company alone."

Felicity threw her head back and laughed. "Look, Faith, I know the two of you have a history, but you don't run my life, and you have no claim on him since you rejected his offer to court. You're old friends and nothing more. That gives you no right to tell me what to do with him."

"I'm sorry if you feel your friendship with him feels a little threatened by my past with him but I wish you wouldn't come to that conclusion." She was prepared to stand her ground with Felicity on the issue, seeing as how her family had become like his own since her father's illness, but he hadn't married into it. She was determined to do whatever she could to get along with Felicity, just short of watching her make a fool of herself by throwing herself shamelessly at Gideon. Still, she couldn't help but be a bit put off by the way her sister was acting toward her, and it wouldn't do either of them any good to allow Gideon to put a wedge between them.

Gideon had been her friend since childhood and her family was always like his own, but did she really want to be with him now that he seemed to be playing a childish game with her sister's heart just to make her jealous? That was not going to make her accept his offer to court her; Faith had sense enough to put her sister first.

"Look, Felicity, I'm not going to argue with you anymore about this; keep your distance from Gideon."

Felicity scowled, planting her hands on her hips. "You have no right to tell me what to do with my own life; I'll do whatever I want. I'm an adult, and not you or anyone can tell me how to run my life."

Faith scoffed at her. "If you're such an adult, why don't you act like one instead of a little school girl because that's how you act around Gideon; it's a little sickening."

"Perhaps you should look at your own actions when you say that, dear *schweschder!*" Felicity narrowed her eyes and walked into the house ahead of her, letting the door slam behind her.

After dinner, Felicity took her turn at washing dishes while their mother helped their father back to bed. He was doing well being up, but it was taking a lot out of him. Faith knew it would take a while before his strength would build up enough to spend more time out of bed than in it.

Gideon left the kitchen and Faith slipped out the front door and went after him, determined to finish her earlier conversation with him. They strolled down to the pond in silence. While they made their way down the path lit up by the moon and stars that shone around the sparse cloud-cover, light snowflakes gently floated down from the heavens and sparkled against the moonlight.

The two of them used to take this same trail down to the pond, from the time they were small children to the time Gideon had tried talking to her about marriage, just before she left for the city. It was the reason she'd left in the first place; perhaps he had scared her by moving too fast and discussing marriage, but that was the way in their community. She often wondered if things would have been different had he held off on the discussion; would she have stayed in the community?

Faith could tell there was something going through Gideon's mind and she could sense it wasn't about her. "What are you thinking about?" she asked, pasting on a smile to hide her annoyance with him.

"Oh, I was thinking of all the times we've worn out this path."

Faith knew that Gideon held a lot of feelings for her, even after all these years, and it made her blood boil that he would risk that by playing along with Felicity's childish game of flirtation.

"What's going on between you and my sister?" she asked, unable to hide the annoyance she felt toward the situation.

"I think you should probably talk to your sister," he said. "I'm not having this conversation with you. My life is no longer any of your business;

you decided that for the both of us when you left the community."

Faith rolled her eyes, making sure Gideon noticed.

"Is there something wrong with that?" He asked.

She shrugged. "You're right about your life being your own business—unless it involves my sister. I don't feel comfortable with how close you two are."

Gideon stopped and looked at her with a serious expression.

"Your family is a big part of my life now that I've been living there for the past six months," he said sternly. "They're very important to me—and that includes you, too—but only as my friend. I've had a lot of years to realize I wanted to court the wrong girl. You've become too *English* for me and don't hold the same attributes I've sought after in a partner."

"And you think my sister is?"

He glared at her. "I would appreciate it if you'd stay out of my business," he said. "You needn't worry about me anymore because it's over between you and me."

Faith left him and walked back to the house, choking back tears she had no intention of shedding.

Chapter 6

Faith kissed her father good night and dragged her tired, cold feet toward her childhood bedroom, pulling her sweater tightly around her. It was cold in the house tonight; the wind whistled through the windows. She turned her head to the side to listen more closely; was that sleigh bells she heard mixed with the whistling wind? She entered her room and crossed to the window, looking down at the yard below.

Clouds covered the moon making it difficult for her to see anything more than shadows, but she could certainly make out a sleigh against the bright snow. She heard the faint thud of the kitchen door closing and saw Felicity running out toward the sleigh. Her heart sped up at the thought of her sister running off and courting someone in secret even though that was the way the youth in the community had always done it. She glared up at the moon, willing the clouds to move so she could catch a glimpse of the driver but it was no use; the sleigh took off in the dark, leaving no clues to his identity.

She sat down on the edge of her bed feeling discouraged and unsure of how she would handle it if she discovered her sister was taking a sleigh ride late at night with Gideon. Would such a thing devastate her? She had tried to mourn over her loss of him earlier—after he'd told her it was over between them. But for some strange reason, she'd been unaffected by it. At least not in the way that she would have expected.

The only way for her to handle her suspicions about the two of them would be to come right out and confront one of them—but which one?

In the morning, Faith stood at her window looking down at the wind-blown tracks the sleigh had made the night before, and it brought new anxiety into her heart. Turning away from the window, she dressed quickly in the dimly lit room and then rushed down the stairs. Thankfully, her mother had not yet entered the kitchen to prepare the morning meal, and so she was able to slip out the door unnoticed.

Wind and snow assaulted her as she made her way in the twilight out to the barn hoping for a little bit of solace to begin the morning chores. Before getting to work, she scooped oats from the barrel and put them in the feedbox for the horses. She busied herself brushing down one of the horses, chatting away like she always did. She loved talking to the animals, and believed it was almost as good as talking to God.

"I bet you think I'm silly for feeling a little jealous over someone I left behind years ago," Faith said to Midnight, her father's horse.

He nickered, and she nuzzled his soft nose.

"Coming home has made me realize that I shouldn't have left all of this behind. I even missed you." She giggled as she hand-fed him some of the oats from the bottom of the bin. Turning to get another scoop of oats, she jumped when she saw Gideon standing behind her.

She clutched her hand to her chest. "Gideon, you scared me; you shouldn't sneak up on me like that."

"I'm sorry, I suppose I'd forgotten how jumpy you always were," he said with a chuckle.

"How was your sleigh ride last night?" She was trying to throw him off what he may have overheard her saying to the horses, and her heart was racing so fast, she thought she may pass out.

"I thought I made it clear to you that what I do on my own time is none of your business," Gideon said.

"It is if it involves my sister," Faith said, trying to hide her anger.

"I had to make a decision to end my pursuit of you; we just don't fit together like I thought we did," Gideon said.

"Yeah, I get that," she snapped at him without meaning to.

Faith couldn't stand the thought of Felicity coming between them, but she would never begrudge her sister's right to happiness.

"Look, Faith, the last thing I want is for things to be awkward between us," he said. "I'm not just working here to help out your family, although it started out that way; I bought into your father's harness-making business and they use that money to pay the medical bills. So, I now own half of that business and I'll be sticking around here. Please don't make this harder for me than it has to be. I care about you; you'll always be a *gut* friend, but that's all there can ever be between us."

Faith caught herself getting choked up about what he'd said and had to turn away from him to hide her emotions. She pretended to keep busy with one of the horses so he wouldn't suspect anything. "I'm sorry; I didn't know about the business," she said, trying to keep her voice as steady as possible. "I guess there's a lot of things I don't know about my own family anymore; I guess I just don't belong here anymore."

She could hear him clearing his throat behind her; it was what he did when he didn't know what to say. Though she remained quiet, her mind raced, but the conclusion was always the same; Gideon was in no position to tell her if there was something between him and Felicity. That was between her and her sister. She had no idea why her sister would not tell her the truth if something was going on, except if she was worried about Faith's feelings. Unfortunately, that didn't make any sense to her either–especially the way Felicity had been acting toward her. Did she fear that Faith would judge her?

Faith couldn't help but wonder if she was the reason Gideon and Felicity were close. One thing she was sure of; she would never get a second chance with him.

Chapter 7

Faith stepped outside the barn and watched a white truck roll up her parents' driveway. She turned to walk back to the barn so she could let Gideon know that his repairman for the *dawdi haus* stove had shown up.

"Faith, is that you?" A somewhat familiar voice said from behind her.

She turned on her heels to face the man who'd gotten out of the work truck. His smile was wide in his handsome face was familiar, but she couldn't quite place him.

"Faith, you don't remember me?" She asked.
"It's me, Mose Yoder!"

She giggled and smiled as he closed the space between them and pulled her into a hug. He quickly pushed her away playfully. "Oh, I'm sorry, I guess I got a little carried away."

She giggled again, her cheeks heating up. "From the look of you," she said. "You've deflected too; you always were a little rebel." His brown, curly hair and chocolate brown eyes set the butterflies in her stomach fluttering.

He laughed. "I'm not the only one. I heard you're a nurse now. I heard about your dad's heart attack; is he doing better now that you're here to take care of him?"

She nodded, pulling her gloved hands to her face to warm her cheeks. "Yes, I'm a nurse, and yes, he's doing a lot better. Thank you for asking." She pointed to his truck. "It looks like you're doing well for yourself; judging by your truck, I'd have to say you probably didn't take the baptism either, am I right?"

He shook his head and lowered his gaze. "After my dad died I needed to get some serious work in order to support my mom and sister," he said. "There just wasn't enough help from the community and the Bishop and I have an understanding about that. I get a lot of work within the community, but most of my business is outside of the community. It was the only way I can keep my family from being homeless."

She put a hand to her mouth and another hand on his arm affectionately. "I'm so sorry about your dad. I'm hoping the Bishop will have just as much grace toward me and my presence here in the community. My circumstances are different, but my services are needed here until my father is well again. It has been hinted around that the community needs a nurse midwife, and I'm giving that some thought."

She hadn't really thought about it until this very moment. It seemed almost comical to her that she would make such a decision based on seeing Mose again.

"I'll understand if you tell me no because of Gideon, but I'm going to be brave and ask you anyway," he said. "Would you like to go for a sleigh ride with me tonight?"

Mose didn't waste any time jumping in with both feet, and she had to admit she was curious, wondering what could be. She liked him; there was no doubt about that.

Faith's breath caught in her throat, her expression slightly stunned, and she could see by his expression it had caused Mose to panic. His question caught her off guard, but she couldn't help thinking that maybe it was time for her to just move on. "I'd love to," she said as quickly as possible, thinking if she didn't get the words out fast they wouldn't come out at all.

"I was hoping you'd like the idea," he said, smiling. "I'm not trying to rush anything. It's just that seeing you back here made me realize how much I missed you."

Faith smiled. "I missed you too. And I would love to go for a sleigh ride with you tonight."

Mose was a good guy, and from where she was standing, his *backbone* looked a lot straighter than Gideon's.

Later that evening, Faith slipped out of the house without being seen and walked to the edge of the driveway to meet Mose. She thought it would be better if they not be seen together by her family just yet in order to avoid having to give any explanations. It wasn't that she was ashamed of any association with him but her family had enough to worry about right now and there was too much bad blood between her and her sister, and now Gideon.

Her boots crunched and squeaked in the snow, and a constant cloud of icy air illuminated by the moonlight came out with each breath she took. She thought her heart would be racing from anticipation, but she felt a comforting sense of calm wash over her at the thought of the night ahead. Like with Gideon, she'd known Mose her whole life, but right now, he seemed to be the only one she had anything in common with. She hadn't felt truly at home since she'd been back, and a sleigh ride with Mose seemed like just the thing to brighten her spirits.

She looked at her watch, another reminder that she no longer fit in with her family or the community, noting that it was eight o'clock—the time they'd agreed upon. Could that have been what Gideon had meant when he'd told her she was no longer a *fit* for him? Had she become too *English* to marry him? If that was the case, she would rather be a spinster than to give up her education and nursing experience for a close-minded man. She was capable of being a nurse, a mother, and a wife—but Gideon would not see it that way. Perhaps their split had been for the best; they'd grown worlds apart, and there would be no closing that gap. He would be better-suited with an Amish woman—a woman like Felicity.

The sound of sleigh bells interrupted her liberating thoughts, and her face lit up when she saw the sleigh come up over the rise. There was something about the moonlight shining on Mose along with the romantic sound of the sleigh bells that made him look as if God had sent him to her.

"Woah," Mose said as he pulled the sleigh up beside Faith. She was happy to see him in full Amish garb since she'd taken the time to iron her best blue dress. He assisted her into the sleigh and draped a blanket over their laps to keep them warm in the icy December air. He snapped the reins and they took off down the path toward Goose Pond behind Hattie King's Bed and Breakfast.

"I'm so glad you agreed to come with me tonight," Mose said. "I was afraid you may have thought I was being too forward and moving too quickly."

Truthfully, Faith hadn't given that too much thought. She knew in her heart that she needed to make some changes in her life, and she trusted God's timing, even if she didn't always understand it.

Faith shrugged and smiled. "I think God has perfect timing."

Mose smiled back, his chiseled jawline peppered with a day's growth of dark whiskers she found very appealing.

As they were approaching the pond that had been frozen over all month, light snow flurries whirled around them. Faith smiled and looked up at the sky, and each snowflake that fell on her seemed to be kissing her cheeks. She had missed moments like this so much while she was away, but it was interesting that she was now experiencing them for the first time with Mose; it almost seemed romantic.

When she'd moved to the city, it was because others who'd come back from their *rumspringa* had convinced her of how magical it was, but she knew those people must never have experienced what she was experiencing right now. There wasn't a single moment she had in the city that could replace this.

Another set of jingle bells startled her; she turned around and looked in the direction of the noise. If she wasn't mistaken, inside the sleigh pulling up at the far side of the pond was Gideon and Felicity.

Chapter 8

Faith was relieved when she saw the sleigh turn around and head back in the direction it had come from. That left her there all alone with Mose, and she was perfectly fine with that.

He helped her out of the sleigh and then reached in the back and handed her two lanterns and grabbed the other two. "I thought we could get some ice skates from the shed up at the B&B and then take a little stroll around the pond. How does that sound?"

Faith hadn't skated since they were younger and she supposed it was just like riding a bike; surely, a person doesn't forget such a thing.

She giggled. "I think that sounds like one of the best ideas I've heard in a long time."

Mose held Faith's hand as they walked up the hill toward the back of the B&B, and the warmth of his hand on hers made her feel tingly—something she'd never experienced before.

The shed sat at the edge of the King's property, but it was a long trek up the hill. Everyone in the community was free to borrow skates if they didn't have their own. Every time there was a skate party, Hattie King would provide everything the youth needed; it had been that way ever since Faith could remember. With Gideon and Felicity now gone, she and Mose would have a good time tonight—at least she hoped they would.

Once they picked out a pair of skates in their sizes, they trudged back down the hill toward the frozen pond. When she put her skates on, Mose lit the lanterns and put them each in a corner of the pond after measuring out ample space for them to skate. With the ice now lit up, he came back and sat beside Faith so he could put his skates on. He quickly laced them up and then pulled a shovel out the back of the sleigh. Faith watched him skate around the pond pushing the shovel to clear the ice. Within minutes, he had managed to push aside the inch or two of snow that had covered the surface of the pond. Now, a shiny sheen of ice sparkled under the lantern lights creating a romantic setting and made Faith feel as giddy as a schoolgirl.

Turn after turn around the pond left Faith's cheeks just as sore as her legs and feet because she just couldn't stop smiling. She couldn't remember the last time she had such a wonderful time just being herself. She'd grown used to being torn between the Amish and English worlds for so long it had begun to wear thin on her nerves. Tonight, she was simply Faith, but she felt like a happy-go-lucky kid again. She was under no pressure to act a certain way around Mose, and because of this, she felt the most relaxed she'd been since she'd come home.

In the morning, Faith went out to the barn to gather the eggs, her constant smile still embedded on her face. It was the first time in a while she'd felt truly happy. In all the years that she'd been away in the city, she'd had a sense of emptiness in her heart and now she felt that it was once again full.

Letting go of Gideon had lifted a weight from her shoulders she had no idea was there—not until Mose pointed it out without saying a single word to her. He'd shown her such a good time last night, and had been so sincere with her, it was like experiencing life for the first time. Thinking back, with Gideon, everything had felt so forced; they were expected to get married, which is probably why he'd asked to court her. She was no more *in love* with him than he was with her. He'd been spot-on yesterday when he'd told her she was not the right fit for him.

Not only did she finally accept it, she fully believed it, and it was a truly liberating concept.

Gideon was busy cleaning out one of the horses' stalls when she walked into the barn.

"Hello Gideon," she said almost too cheerfully.

Gideon jumped, he had been so caught up in his chores he hadn't noticed her come in, and she could tell he was deep in thought.

"You seem really proud of yourself," he said, his tone angry.

She paused for a moment wondering if perhaps he was going to reprimand her for being out with Mose last night, but she knew better. Something had obviously put a thorn in his side and he seemed to be blaming her at the moment.

"What are you talking about," she asked.

He jabbed the pitchfork he been using to pitch clean hay into the stalls into a fresh hay-bail and leaned against the handle. "I'm talking about the way you've been acting ever since you came home," he said angrily. "You come home and start taking control of everything including my life, which you have no business sticking your nose in, and now you ruined everything!"

She was too stunned to talk; what had just happened? What was he blaming her for? Is he really angry with her for coming home? It was her home and not his, but he was acting as if he had a bigger stake in her family than she did. She was only planning on avoiding conversation about seeing them at the pond last night just in case it wasn't time, but now she wanted to know more than ever.

"I only came out here to get eggs for breakfast. I wasn't looking for an argument." She held out a small basket and forced a smile at Gideon, but he ignored her and went back to his chores.

Before Faith could say another word, Felicity walked into the barn with her own basket to collect the eggs. She scrunched up her nose when she saw the two of them together, her lower lip quivered as tears welled up in her eyes.

An alarm went off in Faith's mind; something was seriously wrong with her sister. "I think we need to talk, Felicity."

"I have nothing to say to you." Felicity brushed past her, but whipped her head around and sniffled. "This is all your fault," she cried. "Why did you have to come back here and ruin everything?"

Felicity stormed out of the barn, Faith close on her heels and followed her up to the house. "Why won't you talk to me?" Faith asked. "I'm not a mind reader. I have no idea what's wrong with you unless you tell me."

When Felicity reached the kitchen door she turned around and faced her sister, her face red and blotchy from bawling. "I wish I'd never asked you to come back home," she cried. "You might as well leave because I don't care if I ever see you again!"

Chapter 9

Faith didn't know what to do with herself; she usually cooked when she was upset, but this was more upset than she'd ever been in her life. She went into the kitchen hoping that busying herself would take her mind off her troubles. She'd not said a word in the last thirty minutes, and for the first time in her life, she was at a loss for words. Sobs tried to make their way up her throat but she swallowed them down.

She set to work gathering ingredients for breakfast while her mother began the bread-making.

She looked in the small refrigerator that was powered by their generator, not finding any fresh buttermilk for the pancakes she'd had her heart set on making.

"If you're looking for buttermilk," her mother said over her shoulder. "You'll have to look in the cellar."

Her mother knew her well and it was a good thing. It often came in handy to help keep her on task. She left the other ingredients on the counter in the kitchen and went to the mudroom where the entrance to the cellar was. She grabbed a match from the box near the door and struck it to light the lantern. Holding onto the rail, she descended the creaky steps until her feet touched the dirt floor below. She stretched out her arm in front of her that held the lantern and surveyed the many shelves and bins. She searched until her gaze stopped at the far corner where several bins contained enough celery for a very large—*wedding!*

Her breath hitched at the reality that suddenly hit her like a large rock smacking her in the head. It was all beginning to make sense now: the wedding ring pattern quilt, the sleigh rides, exchanged glances across the dinner table. Her sister's giggling and flirting when she was around Gideon was more than just flirting or a school-girl crush—she was in love with him.

Then the reality hit her; her mother knew she needed to see it for herself.

Felicity was marrying *her* Gideon.

No wonder they're both so angry with me!

"When were you going to tell me about you and Gideon, Felicity?" Faith demanded. "On your twenty-fifth wedding anniversary?"

"If you must know, I was hoping you'd leave after Christmas and I wouldn't have to deal with you and your jealousy!"

"I'm not jealous!" Faith said. "But the truth would have been nice to hear."

Felicity planted her hands on her hips. "I don't owe you any explanation for my life; when you left here, you left your *familye* behind. *Ach,* you don't look or act Amish anymore; you're like a stranger to me."

Their mother poked her head out the door where their father was obviously sleeping, and hushed the two of them. "I'm not sure what's gotten into the two of you, their mother said. "But I have a pretty *gut* idea, and the two of you need to settle your differences, and do it quickly and quietly so your *daed* doesn't hear you."

Faith's expression fell. Her mother was right about all of it but that didn't change the fact that this would likely get worse before it got better. They had a long history of childish spats but this was much more than that; this was grown up stuff and those problems weren't always easy to fix. She nodded to her mother and waited for her to close the door before resuming her conversation with Felicity.

"What's wrong?" she asked again. "Do I have to say it for you, or are you going to act like a grown woman who is about to be married, and tell me the truth?"

Felicity's eyes widened and she swiped at the tears with the backs of her hands.

"This isn't like you," Felicity said, turning her back to her. "The Faith I know would never treat me like such a child, and she wouldn't get in the middle of my relationship out of jealousy, or shamelessly throw herself at Gideon. The Faith I knew had a lot more dignity than that. I guess the city got to you more than I thought."

Faith's jaw dropped; she couldn't believe her sister would say something so hurtful. She was only standing up for herself against Felicity. Her eyes began to well up with tears.

"I wasn't throwing myself at him," she said, her tone defensive. "Before you interrupted me out there in the barn earlier, I had planned to tell him he was released from his obligation to marry me."

Mere minutes ago, she felt proud of herself for making the decision to move forward and to let

Gideon go. She felt as if she'd won a small victory, but now it was obvious she lost a friend and had unknowingly destroyed her relationship with her sister. How had things managed to get so out of control? It amazed her how what she had envisioned for this family visit had become so far the opposite of what it had become in reality.

Felicity twisted up her face. "You think he feels obligated to you? Why, because you have a history of *friendship*? Because as far as I know, that's all it ever was between the two of you."

Faith realized that her sister was right in some respects, she hadn't acted with dignity when she'd first arrived, thinking she could rekindle a lost cause with Gideon. Maybe the city had changed her some, but not so much that she would deliberately hurt her sister.

"I'm sorry, Felicity," she said. "I know there are no words for my behavior but I was confused when I came home and I treated you like a little sister instead of a grown woman."

Felicity sobbed. "I don't care what you have to say, Faith. I don't care about anything anymore; none of it matters because I called off the wedding!"

Chapter 10

"All I want to know is; do you love her?" Faith questioned Gideon.

He nodded and smiled sadly. "Of course, I do, but she broke it off with me and said she won't marry me unless we get your blessing."

Faith guffawed. "*My blessing?* That's usually reserved for the *father* of the bride—not the sister!"

"Yes, but she doesn't want to hurt you. Don't you see? She doesn't want me to come between the two of you. So, you *must* give us your blessing, or she'll never agree to marry me now."

Faith sighed heavily. How had she managed to get herself into such a dilemma? At the same time, how could she refuse a simple request from her friend for her sister?

She smiled genuinely. "I'm sorry; I'll tell her she has my blessing."

He was so excited he pulled Faith into a hug, but it was interrupted by a squeal and a cry from Felicity.

"How could you?" she cried.

She ran out of the barn and Faith ran after her. When she caught up to her, she had tears in her eyes and she was shaking.

Snow blew around them, whipping the hems of their dresses, but Faith didn't care how cold she was; she was going to settle this with her sister once and for all.

"Don't tell me you aren't throwing yourself at Gideon because I just saw you hugging him!" she squealed.

Faith laughed. "You've got it all wrong, little sister!" she said, unable to stop from laughing.

"I'm so glad you find it funny to steal my betrothed from me!" Felicity sobbed.

"I wasn't throwing myself at him and he can't be stolen from you; he loves you!" Faith said. "He wants to marry you—and you have *my blessing.*"

That calmed her down.

She wiped her tears and threw her arms around Faith, giggles erupting from her.

"Do you mean it?"

She held her sister close; she never thought she'd ever beg to have her chatty sister talking to her but that was next if she hadn't made up her mind to finally listen to reason.

"You march out to that barn and tell that man you'll marry him—and that your sister will be standing up with you at the wedding—that is, if you'll have me!" Faith pushed out her lower lip and tried not to giggle.

Faith readied herself for her date with Mose; they'd been seeing each other every opportunity they could for the past week. He'd offered to take her somewhere out to dinner in his truck, but she'd opted for another sleigh ride by moonlight, complete with a basket of baked-goods and a large thermos full of hot cocoa.

She had told him to bring the sleigh up the driveway; this time she had no reason to hide her meeting with him. Felicity had never been so excited for her when she'd shared her news with her sister. Faith, however, was more excited for Felicity and her upcoming wedding on New Year's Day.

When the sound of sleigh bells entered her ears, she hurried out the door, feeling giddy like a teenager during *rumspringa*. She watched him drive the horse up the snowy driveway, icy puffs of air rolling from the horse's nostrils, a wreath of bells hanging from his neck.

He assisted her into the sleigh and climbed up beside her, tucking the lap quilt around her. He put an arm around her causing her to giggle inwardly, his closeness heating her cold cheeks. He tapped the reins on the horse's hindquarters and the sleigh lurched forward down the snowy path that led out to the country road. She was content to ride in silence next to him, the romantic jingle bells adding magic to their night together.

When they reached the pond, they were all alone. She leaned back in the seat and rested her head on his shoulder while he pointed out a shooting star. She made a wish as it soared across the sky, that God would show her if Mose was the right man for her. She felt it in her heart, but she was scared to follow anything but God's prompting. She'd already made the mistake of thinking she knew what her future was supposed to be. Those mistakes had almost cost her the family God had finally reunited her with.

"I can't believe it's Christmas Eve," she said, as he helped her out of the sleigh.

"I have a gift for you," Mose said, pulling a small box from his pocket and handing it to her.

Faith giggled as she reached for the box and opened it. Her breath caught in her throat, her emotions bringing tears of joy to her eyes as she looked upon the polished red stone in the shape of a heart.

"Faith," he said. "That's stone represents me giving my heart to you if you'll have it."

She was so caught up in the moment that she laughed and cried at the same time. "Yes, I'll have your heart if you'll have mine."

He pulled her into his arms and pressed his lips to hers, snowflakes billowing around them and landing on their warm cheeks.

Faith listened intently as her father read the story of Christ's birth from the Bible and then they bowed their heads for the Christmas prayer.

He sliced the large turkey while everyone else passed sweet bread, *chowchow*, dumplings and gravy, beets, and much more.

Conversations erupted around the table, but her mother hadn't yet let go of her hand since the prayer; she gave it a little squeeze.

"I'm so happy you're with us this Christmas," she said.

Faith smiled, a lump forming in her throat. "I wouldn't have missed this for anything; I'm sorry it took me so long to come home, *Mamm.*"

Her mother smiled; she hadn't called her *mamm* since she'd been back. "All is forgiven if I can talk you into moving back home," she said.

This was where her heart belonged; for the first time since she'd left the city to return to the Amish community, she finally felt at home. Did she want to stay and return to the Amish way of life?

The answer was yes.

Faith leaned her head on her mother's shoulder, gazing at each of her loved-ones around the table. Her father had been taking his meals with them all week; his strength had increased and he even made it out to the barn with Gideon a couple of times. Mose, who sat next to her, had just become a part of her future. Never in a million years would she have thought she could sit at a table with Gideon as part of her family unless he was marrying her. She giggled inwardly at how things had turned out. Her childhood friend was never meant to be her husband; only God knew he was destined to be her brother-in-law.

Then her eyes met with Felicity's. She smiled, and it brought so much joy to her heart she felt it might burst.

"*Jah!* I'm going to stay, *mamm,*" Faith answered. "This is my home."

THE END

You might also like…

His Amish Baby: Book One

Amish Dynasty Collection

Newly Released books
99 cents or FREE with
Kindle Unlimited.

♡ LOVE to Read?
♡ LOVE 99 cent Books?
♡ LOVE GIVEAWAYS?

SIGN UP NOW
Click the Link Below to Join
my Exclusive Mailing List

PLEASE SIGN UP on FACEBOOK!

Please follow me on Facebook

Made in the USA
Middletown, DE
08 December 2017